I Want to Be
A
BALLET DANCER

By Liza Alexander
Illustrated by Carol Nic

D1517254

A SESAME STREET/GOLDEN BOOK
Published by Western Publishing Company, Inc.,
in conjunction with Children's Television Workshop.

© 1993 Children's Television Workshop. Jim Henson's Sesame Street Muppet Characters © 1993 Jim Henson Productions, Inc. All rights reserved. Printed in the U.S.A. No part of this book may be reproduced or copied in any form without written permission from the copyright owner. Sesame Street and the Sesame Street Sign are trademarks and service marks of Children's Television Workshop. All other trademarks are the property of Western Publishing Company, Inc. Library of Congress Catalog Card Number: 92-74563 ISBN: 0-307-13121-1/ISBN: 0-307-63121-4 (lib. bdg.) A MCMXCIII

Hello! My name is Prairie Dawn. Every Tuesday and Thursday I take ballet class. I come to the studio early so I can see the end of the class for the big boys and girls.

I love to watch the big girls put on their toe shoes. The toe shoes have satiny ribbons. The big girls look so pretty when they glide across the floor on their tippy toes!

We change clothes in the dressing room. I wear a leotard and tights and tie my hair back off my face, just like the big girls do. I have little pink ballet slippers, but I am still too small to dance in toe shoes. I must wait until I am eleven or twelve and my bones and muscles are stronger.

It is time for our class to begin. First we warm up at the barre. The barre is a pole attached along the wall. We hold on to it to keep our balance.

We start each class with pliés. We look in the mirrors to check that we are doing our best. A piano player plays for us. We must listen very carefully so we can dance in time to the music.

After our warm-up at the barre, we go to the middle of the floor. We practice the five positions of the feet and arms:

first position . . .

second position . . .

third . . .

fourth . . .

and fifth!

Sometimes we learn new steps. Today we are trying pirouettes. A pirouette is a twirl. We can't do pirouettes very well yet, but Miss Natalia says, "Practice makes perfect pirouettes!"

We are also working on little jumps
called changements. Here I go. . . .

See! I am quite good at changements.

Now comes my favorite part of ballet class—big leaps!
We run, jump, stretch our legs out in a split, and soar
through the air like birds.

At the end of class we do our reverence.
Reverence is a fancy curtsy, which we do
to thank the piano player, our teacher,
and ourselves.

I am very happy! Miss Natalia has asked me to help with the little kids' class. I will be a good helper. I took the class when I was little, and I remember everything.

The tiny dancers do not use the barre. They are too small. They sit in a circle on the floor instead. We teach them the five positions and how to count to the music.

Miss Natalia is always saying, "Children! Pull in your tummies!" Or "Children, keep your backs straight! Pretend there is a glass of water on top of your head, and try not to spill it!"

At the end of the class we ask the tiny dancers to twirl like snowflakes and hop like bunny rabbits!

Herry and I go to a performance of the Sesame Street Ballet. Miss Natalia gave me tickets to thank me for helping her. Miss Natalia herself is dancing! She is a member of the ballet company.

The ballet is perfectly beautiful! It tells a story in music and dance instead of words.

After the ballet we go backstage. Miss Natalia looks
very happy but tired. The dancers make ballet look easy,
but we dancers know that ballet can be hard work!
　　Herry wants to know if he can be a ballet dancer
someday.

Miss Natalia smiles and says, "Just maybe, Herry, if you keep taking classes and work hard. But you'll have to study ballet for many years. Only the very best dancers can become members of ballet companies."

Then Miss Natalia unties her toe shoes and takes them off. She signs her name twice, right on the toes, and gives the toe shoes to me to keep! This is the most exciting moment of my life . . . because when I grow up, I want to be a ballet dancer.